Kitty Cat, Kitty Cat,
Are You Waking Up?

BY Bill Martin Jr and Michael Sampson

ILLUSTRATED BY Laura J. Bryant

two lions

two lions

Amazon Publishing
Attn: Amazon Children's Publishing, P.O. Box 400818, Las Vegas, NV 89140
www.amazon.com/amazonchildrenspublishing

Library of Congress Cataloging-in-Publication Data
Martin, Bill, 1916–2004.
Kitty Cat, Kitty Cat, are you waking up? / by Bill Martin Jr. & Michael Sampson; illustrated by Laura J. Bryant. — 1st ed.
p. cm.
Summary: Kitty Cat is distracted by many things as she gets ready for school in the morning.
ISBN 978-0-7614-5841-8 (paperback)
[1. Stories in rhyme. 2. Cats—Fiction.] I. Sampson, Michael R. II. Bryant, Laura J., ill. III. Title.
PZ8.3.M3988Ki 2008
[E]—dc22
2007041987

The illustrations are rendered in watercolor paints
and colored pencils on Strathmore paper.
Book design by Anahid Hamparian
Editor: Margery Cuyler
Printed in China

To my cat-loving niece, Leslie
—M.S.

To the many kitty cats that have napped on my lap
—L.J.B.

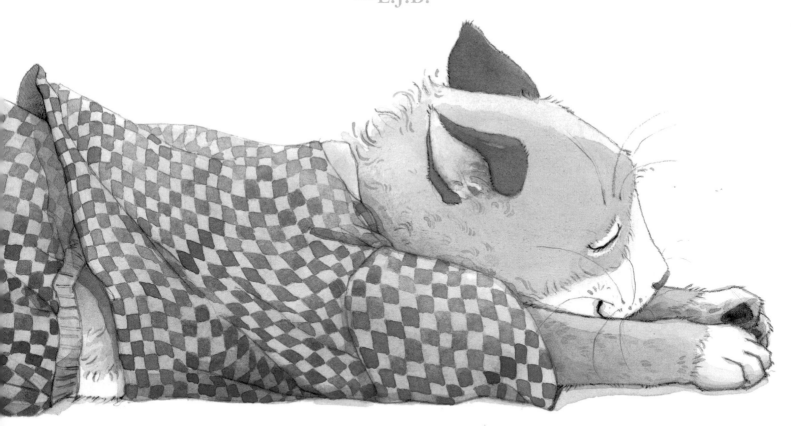

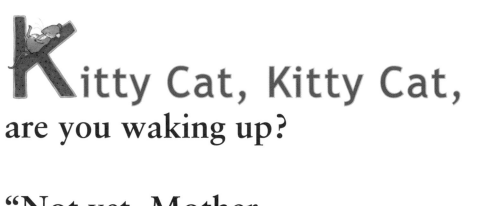**K**itty Cat, Kitty Cat,
are you waking up?

"Not yet, Mother,
I'm a sleepy buttercup."

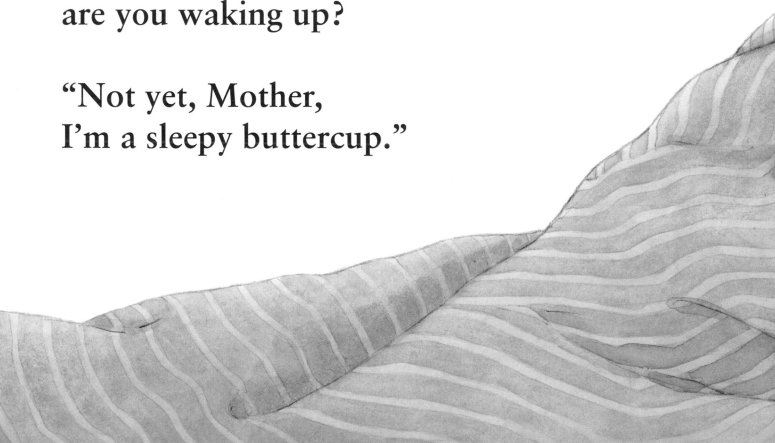

"Kitty Cat, Kitty Cat,
are you out of bed?"

"Not yet, Mother,
I'm standing on my head."

"Kitty Cat, Kitty Cat,
have you cleaned your fur?"

"Not yet, Mother,
I'm practicing my purr."

"Kitty Cat, Kitty Cat,
what are you going to wear?"

"Just a second, Mother,
I'm looking everywhere."

"Kitty Cat, Kitty Cat,
where'd you put your socks?"

"Just a second, Mother,
they're over by my blocks."

"Kitty Cat, Kitty Cat,

have you found your shoes?"

"Just a second, Mother,

they're easy things to lose."

"Kitty Cat, Kitty Cat,
do you want some fish?"

"Just a second, Mother,
I'm playing with my dish."

"Kitty Cat, Kitty Cat,
hurry up and eat."

"Just a second, Mother,
a mouse is on my seat!"

"Kitty Cat, Kitty Cat,
you'll be very late!"

"Just a second, Mother,
school will have to wait."

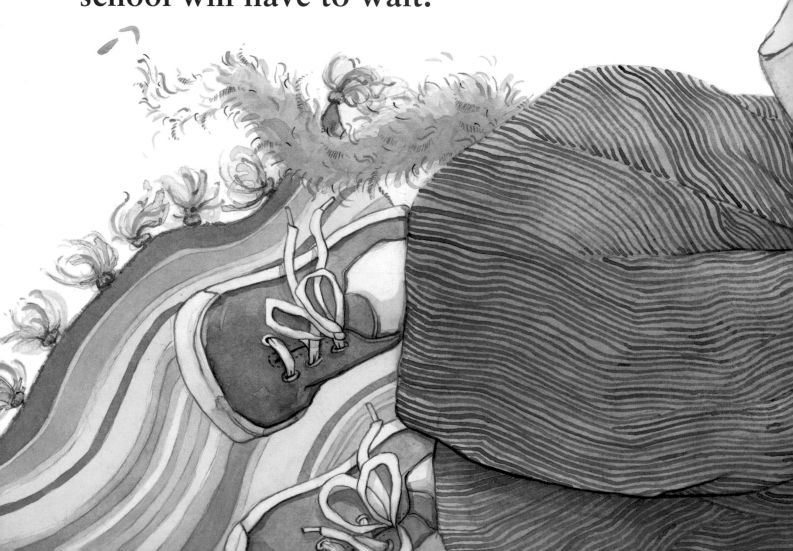

"Kitty Cat, Kitty Cat,
now we have to go!"

"Okay, Mother,
I'm sorry I'm so slow."